BOOK SOLD
NO LONGER R.H.P.L.
PROPERTY

D1126941

[SURVIVING THE IMPOSSIBLE]

SURVIVING
AN ALIEN INVASION

CHARLIE OGDEN

Gareth Stevens
PUBLISHING

Please visit our website, **www.garethstevens.com**.
For a free color catalog of all our high-quality books,
call toll free 1-800-542-2595 or fax 1-877-542-2596.

CATALOGING-IN-PUBLICATION DATA

Names: Ogden, Charlie.
Title: Surviving an alien invasion / Charlie Ogden.
Description: New York : Gareth Stevens Publishing, 2018. | Series: Surviving the impossible |
    Includes index.
Identifiers: ISBN 9781538214619 (pbk.) | ISBN 9781538214183 (library bound) | ISBN 9781538214626
    (6 pack)
Subjects: LCSH: Human-alien encounters--Juvenile literature. | Disasters--Juvenile literature. |
    Survival--Juvenile literature.
Classification: LCC BF2050.O43 2018 | DDC 001.942--dc23

Published in 2018 by
Gareth Stevens Publishing
111 East 14th Street, Suite 349
New York, NY 10003

Copyright © 2018 BookLife

Written by: Charlie Ogden
Edited by: Kirsty Holmes
Designed by: Drue Rintoul

Photo credits: Abbreviations: l–left, r–right, b–bottom, t–top, c–center, m–middle. Images are courtesy
of Shutterstock.com. With thanks to Getty Images, Thinkstock Photo and iStockphoto. 2 – solarseven.
3 – Traveller Martin. 4 – Vadim Sadovski. 5t – Aphelleon. 5b – FooTToo. 7tr – GG Holy Ghost Panel, by
John Fowler, via WikimediaCommons. 8t – Fer Gregory. 8b – canbedone. 9 – Fer Gregory. 9bm – adike.
10 – Vadim Sadovski. 11t – pixelparticle. 11b – sdecoret. 11br – Sarah Holmlund. 12 – Vadim Sadovsk.
13t – Sean Pavone & Chromatika Multimedia snc. 13b – Fer Gregory. 15t – Made by X51 (Flickr: http://
www.flickr.com/photos/x51/ Web: http://x51.org/) [GFDL (http://www.gnu.org/copyleft/fdl.html) or CC-
BY-SA-3.0 (http://creativecommons.org/licenses/by-sa/3.0/)], via Wikimedia Commons. 15b – AlexLMX
& adike. 16t – Lena_graphics. 16b – Marina Sun. 17bl – Leo Blanchette. 18t – Sarah Holmlund. 18b – Denise
LeBlanc. 19 – Lena_graphics & Tatiana Popova. 20 – Vinne & Sarah Holmlund. 21t – First Step Studio. 21b –
ANIMACIONMX. 22b – First Step Studio. 23 – Mopic. 24 – Alexyz3d. 25tr – IgorXIII. 25b – Fotokvadra. 26t
– Juergen Faelchle. 26b – Marc Ward. 27t – JasaStyle. 27b – tinta. 28 – mario.bono. 29t – Iakov Kalinin.
29b – Christopher Wood. 30t – Pixus.

All rights reserved. No part of this book may be reproduced in any
form without permission from the publisher, except by a reviewer.

Printed in China
CPSIA compliance information: Batch CW18GS: For further information contact
Gareth Stevens, New York, New York at 1-800-542-2595.

RICHMOND HILL PUBLIC LIBRARY
32972001036427 **RG**
Surviving an alien invasion
Jul. 27, 2018

CONTENTS

Words that look like THIS can be found in the glossary on page 31.

THE ALIENS ARE COMING

While some people hold onto the belief that aliens aren't real, a lot of people are certain they are. How can we be the only ones in this vast, endless universe? Sure, Earth is very lucky. We are just the right distance from the Sun, have just the right gases in our ATMOSPHERE, and, most importantly, have just the right amount of water to support life.

But surely we can't be the only place in the universe that is like this. There are billions of planets in each GALAXY, and billions of galaxies in the universe. Even if only 0.00000000001% of the planets in the universe are capable of supporting life, there will be hundreds – if not thousands – of alien species out there!

Assuming that there are at least some alien species – would they come to Earth? Well, at least they will know where we are. For decades, humans have been sending RADIO SIGNALS into space. These signals could be picked up by aliens far outside the solar system. If an alien CIVILIZATION picked up just one of these signals, it wouldn't take them long to figure out where we are.

ANCIENT SIGNS OF ALIENS

Not only does it seem likely that alien civilizations are out there, it also seems possible that they have been visiting Earth for thousands of years. By studying **ANCIENT** pieces of art, we can see mysterious signs that suggest aliens might have visited people in the past.

Some of the earliest signs of aliens visiting people on Earth come from cave paintings. Cave paintings throughout Europe, some of which are over 10,000 years old, seem to show alien beings of different kinds wearing space suits. Obviously, this was thousands of years before humans developed space suits, so how did these ancient people know what a space suit looked like? Some people believe it's a sign that aliens visited the people who made these paintings.

Many people believe that the Egyptians were the first human civilization to be visited by aliens. By studying Egyptian hieroglyphics, some people have come to the conclusion that the ancient civilization was visited by – and helped by – beings from another world. This could help explain why the Egyptians were so much more ADVANCED than other civilizations at the time.

Egyptian hieroglyphs seem to show pharaohs standing beside alien spaceships and modern TECHNOLOGY. Some people believe this technology could only have been shown to the Egyptians by aliens.

MODERN SIGNS OF ALIENS

Just as there are signs that alien beings visited people in the past, there are also many recent events that some people believe are signs of alien visits.

Crop circles are huge patterns and shapes that appear in fields, usually overnight. While we know that humans are responsible for many of these crop circles, some are still left unexplained. How did they get there? Well, some people believe that they are the marks left over by alien spaceships landing on Earth. The patterns are so complicated, yet so perfect. Who else could make them besides advanced alien beings?

On top of this, there are many stories from people who claim to have been abducted, or kidnapped, by aliens. Many of the stories have a lot of things in common – bright lights in the sky, being pulled up by a mysterious light, being held on an alien spaceship, and then being returned to Earth a few days later. Some people believe that these abduction stories are proof that aliens are coming to Earth and studying humans.

Fact: Hundreds of people from around the world claim to have been abducted by aliens.

THE INVASION

With all these spooky mysteries, it seems like aliens could attack at any moment. You need to be prepared so that when they do invade, you'll be ready. In the days and weeks leading up to an alien INVASION, there will be signs that beings from another world are on their way. Most people won't notice these signs because they won't know what to look out for – but you will.

METEORITES

One of the most obvious signs of an impending alien invasion is METEORITES falling to Earth. Of course, they won't actually be meteorites – they will just look like them. In reality, the objects falling to Earth could be small alien spaceships or pieces of alien technology that will help the aliens once they begin their invasion. Most people – including scientists – will insist that these are just falling space rocks. But you will know better.

LIGHTS IN THE SKY

If these "meteorites" are accompanied by strange, colorful lights in the night sky, then you can be pretty certain that an alien invasion is about to begin. The lights in the sky will actually be distant alien spaceships that are speeding towards Earth, closer and closer. Watch out for these lights and listen for strange humming noises coming from the sky. This could be a sign that the spaceships are preparing to land and the invasion is only days – or perhaps only hours – away from starting.

WHEN YOU KNOW FOR SURE

The first people to know for absolute certain that an alien invasion is upon us will probably be astronauts. Being up in space already, these brave explorers will probably be the first people to see alien spaceships moving towards Earth. Hopefully they will have enough time to send a warning to us down on Earth, letting us know that an invasion is about to begin.

ALIEN SPACESHIPS

After whizzing past the INTERNATIONAL SPACE STATION and diving through Earth's atmosphere, the aliens may well park their spaceships in our skies and wait, hovering, for a few days. During this time, they will most likely be studying Earth and us humans, figuring out who's in charge, what resources they can steal, and where to attack first.

On the other hand, the aliens might land their spaceships on the ground. This could help them to get a closer look at the planet, study what the Earth is made of, and give them a better position to attack from. Whether they wait in the sky or crash straight down to Earth, one thing is for certain – you'll need to pack your bags and head somewhere safe.

Top Tip: Alien spaceships could look completely different from the pictures shown here. Expect the unexpected.

PLACES TO AVOID

If the aliens are coming to take over Earth and EXTERMINATE all the people living here, then they will want to target the places where the most people live. So, until you know whether the aliens come in peace or not, there are a few places that you should avoid.

LOCKED ON

WORLD CITIES

If the aliens are planning to take over the world and destroy all humans, it will make sense for them to attack world cities first. The biggest and most important cities will become targets. They are:

- New York, USA
- London, England
- Berlin, Germany
- Tokyo, Japan
- Mexico City, Mexico
- Istanbul, Turkey
- Moscow, Russia
- Delhi, India
- Seoul, South Korea
- Toronto, Canada
- Karachi, Pakistan
- Lagos, Nigeria
- Beijing, China
- Cairo, Egypt
- Rio de Janeiro, Brazil
- Buenos Aires, Argentina.

If you live in any of these cities, get out fast.

Another place that it is very important to avoid is Area 51. Area 51 is an American Air Force base in Nevada. It is highly classified, meaning that the United States **GOVERNMENT** does not share any information about what goes on there and almost no one is allowed to go there in person. Because Area 51 is such a secret, many people suspect that it is where the United States government studies alien technology and aliens that have come to Earth. It's possible that aliens are being kept in Area 51 against their will. If this is the case, the aliens might be invading Earth to break their friends out of prison.

WE COME IN PEACE

But wait. Let's hold on a second. It might not be the case that the aliens have come to take over Earth and exterminate all the stupid humans who think they own the place. Maybe, just maybe, they really have come in peace.

MATH AND SCIENCE

After all, us humans are pretty incredible. We have very large, very complicated brains that are capable of understanding everything from love and tragedy to QUANTUM MECHANICS and brain surgery. Maybe the aliens have come to Earth to learn a thing or two.

If this is the case, what could we teach them? Well, we know a lot about the universe — we have a good idea about how it began and how planets and STARS are formed. We could explain to them the process of EVOLUTION and help them understand how life on Earth works. Maybe the aliens have come to learn, not to destroy.

Fact: The aliens must be pretty clever if they've made it all the way to Earth, but it is possible that they haven't discovered everything that humans have discovered.

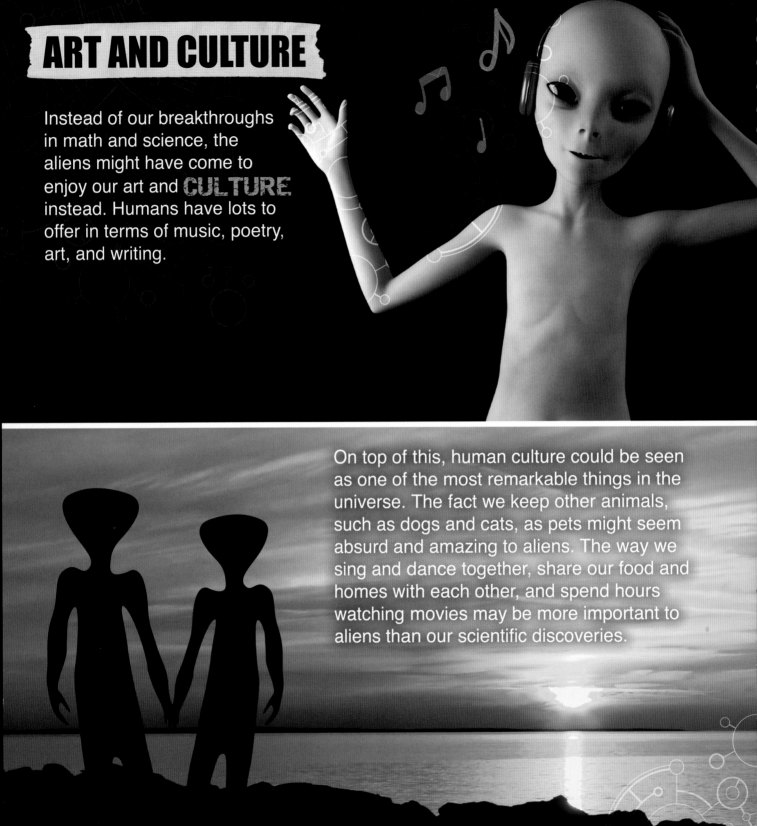

ART AND CULTURE

Instead of our breakthroughs in math and science, the aliens might have come to enjoy our art and CULTURE instead. Humans have lots to offer in terms of music, poetry, art, and writing.

On top of this, human culture could be seen as one of the most remarkable things in the universe. The fact we keep other animals, such as dogs and cats, as pets might seem absurd and amazing to aliens. The way we sing and dance together, share our food and homes with each other, and spend hours watching movies may be more important to aliens than our scientific discoveries.

We have no idea what life is like for alien beings. What seems normal to us may be the most amazing thing in the universe to them. Our oceans and sandy beaches may make Earth seem like a great vacation destination. Perhaps they just wanted to get away from the stresses of intergalactic space travel? They may even have traveled all this way just to watch human TV shows!

19

THE NEXT STAGE OF HUMAN EVOLUTION

If the aliens that come to Earth are friendly, they may lead to the next stage in human evolution! To get to Earth in the first place, the aliens' rocket technology will have to be a lot better than ours. While humans know a lot about science and math, it would still take us decades to reach the edge of the solar system in a spaceship.

The aliens will be from another solar system entirely, or maybe even from another galaxy. In order to travel so far, they must have some pretty amazing technology. If they share this technology with us, it may change everything about the way we live our lives.

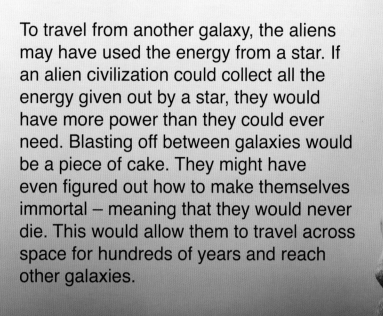

To travel from another galaxy, the aliens may have used the energy from a star. If an alien civilization could collect all the energy given out by a star, they would have more power than they could ever need. Blasting off between galaxies would be a piece of cake. They might have even figured out how to make themselves immortal – meaning that they would never die. This would allow them to travel across space for hundreds of years and reach other galaxies.

If the aliens are friendly and decide to share their technology with us humans, it could solve a lot of the world's problems. If we could collect more of the energy given out by the Sun, everyone could have free energy, and we could use this to make enough food to feed everyone on the planet. If the aliens are friendly, it could be the best thing that ever happened to us. However, that is a big "if," because the aliens might not be friendly at all...

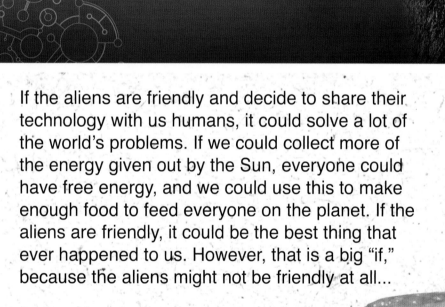

EVIL ALIENS

If the aliens are not friendly, we are going to have a lot of problems. With their advanced technology, it is unlikely that the human race will be able to do much to stop them if they want to destroy us. However, there are a number of things you can do to prepare yourself for the invasion. First, you need to figure out why the aliens have come.

RESOURCES:
- BASE METALS
- BASE GASES
- PRECIOUS STONES
- WATER
- FOSSIL FUELS
- HUMANS

If the aliens have not come in peace, then it's likely that they've come to take Earth's natural resources. The Earth has many resources, such as rocks, metals, and gemstones, which the aliens might want to take for themselves and their buddies back on their home planet. However, these resources can be found on many other planets in the universe. If the aliens have come to Earth, they have probably come for the resources that are harder to find elsewhere – such as FOSSIL FUELS, water, and … humans.

Fact: Humans could be a very useful resource to aliens. With our powerful brains and our ability to work together, they might want to take us as slaves for their alien civilization.

HUMANITY MUST WORK TOGETHER

If HUMANITY is going to survive, we are all going to have to work together. Any one country has a slim chance of defeating an invading, evil, resource-hungry alien civilization all by itself. However, maybe – just maybe – if we all work together, we might stand a chance at fighting them off. If all 7.5 billion people on planet Earth work together, we could achieve great things.

The world contains a LOT of weapons. If every country in the world decided to share all its weapons, we would have enough guns and rockets to destroy a lot of alien spaceships... Probably. It's very hard to know for sure. There is no way of knowing how advanced the alien technology will be, so there's no way of knowing if our weapons would do anything at all.

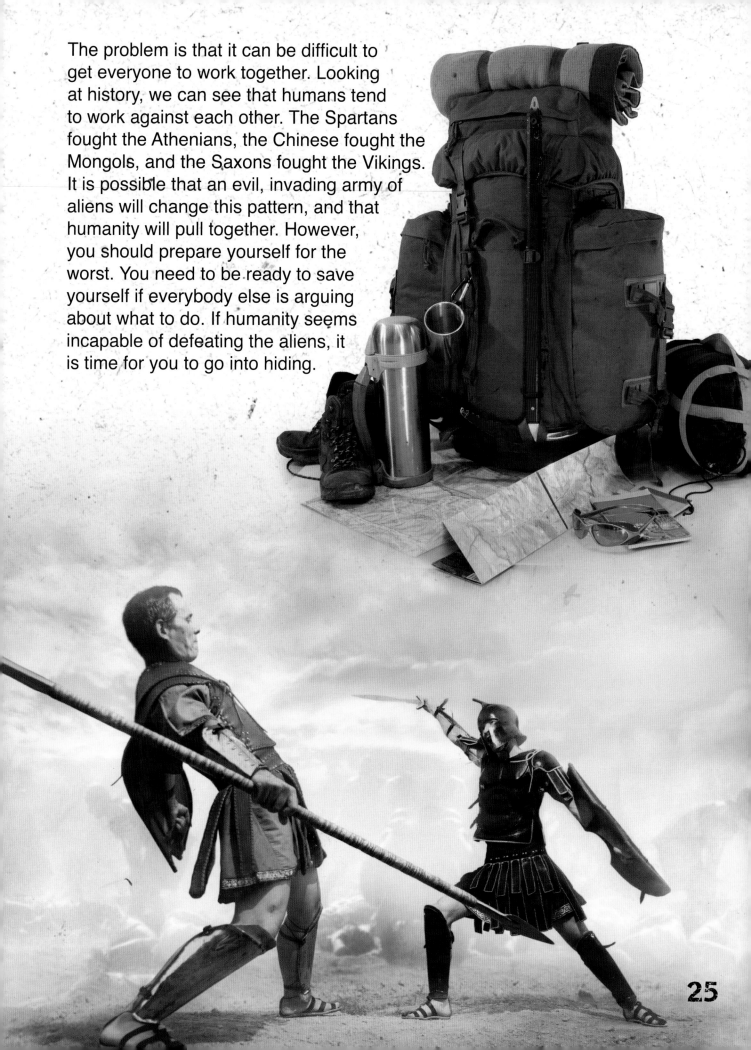

The problem is that it can be difficult to get everyone to work together. Looking at history, we can see that humans tend to work against each other. The Spartans fought the Athenians, the Chinese fought the Mongols, and the Saxons fought the Vikings. It is possible that an evil, invading army of aliens will change this pattern, and that humanity will pull together. However, you should prepare yourself for the worst. You need to be ready to save yourself if everybody else is arguing about what to do. If humanity seems incapable of defeating the aliens, it is time for you to go into hiding.

25

CHOOSING A HIDEOUT

Finding a suitable **HIDEOUT** to escape the evil aliens is going to be very, very difficult. Very few places on Earth will be outside the watchful eye of the aliens. With their advanced technology, they might be able to scan any area for signs of useful resources or human life.

SCANNING FOR HUMANS
— RESULTS: OVER 7,500,000,000

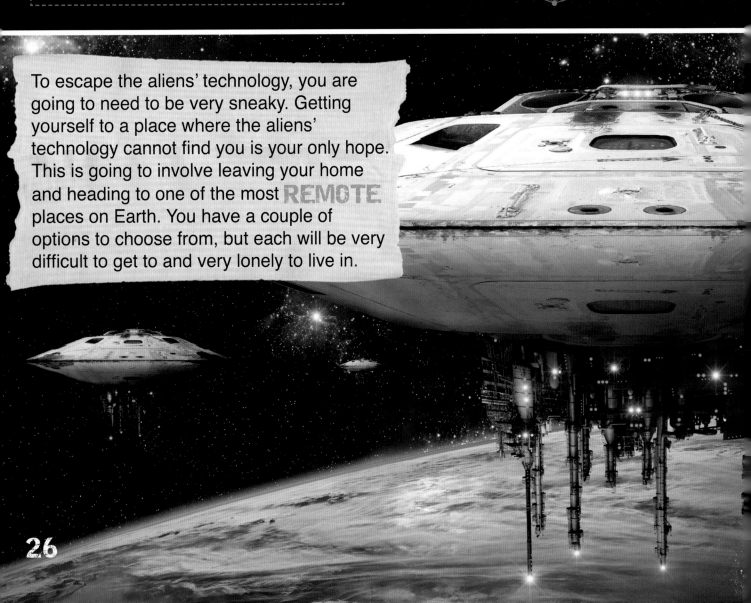

To escape the aliens' technology, you are going to need to be very sneaky. Getting yourself to a place where the aliens' technology cannot find you is your only hope. This is going to involve leaving your home and heading to one of the most **REMOTE** places on Earth. You have a couple of options to choose from, but each will be very difficult to get to and very lonely to live in.

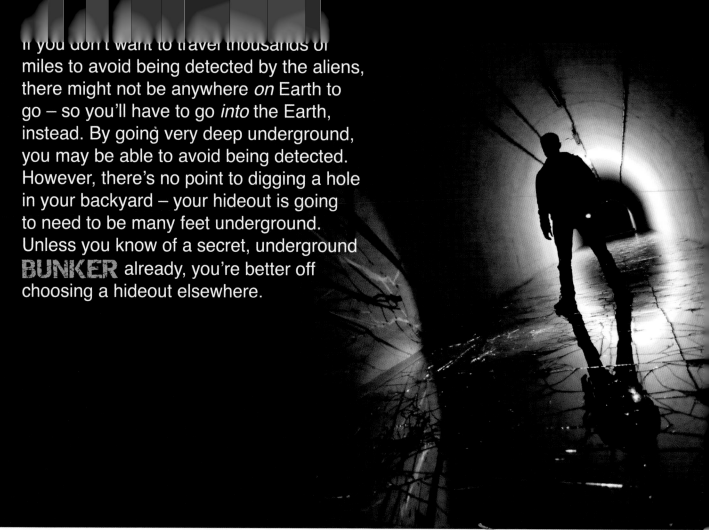

If you don't want to travel thousands of miles to avoid being detected by the aliens, there might not be anywhere *on* Earth to go – so you'll have to go *into* the Earth, instead. By going very deep underground, you may be able to avoid being detected. However, there's no point to digging a hole in your backyard – your hideout is going to need to be many feet underground. Unless you know of a secret, underground **BUNKER** already, you're better off choosing a hideout elsewhere.

JUNGLES, DESERTS, AND THE ARCTIC

If you can't find yourself a comfy underground bunker to hide in, you are best off thinking about what resources the aliens have come to find on Earth. If you know what the aliens are looking for, you can avoid places where these things can be found. This will help you to avoid being abducted for as long as possible, but it is unlikely to keep you safe forever.

If the aliens are looking for water, then your best chance at avoiding being found is to go somewhere without much water. In this situation, a desert is a good option. The aliens are unlikely to scan desert areas for water, as they could find large amounts of water more easily in other places. However, hiding in the desert comes with its own challenges — mainly, not having enough water! If you are going to survive in the desert, you are going to need to find an oasis.

Fact: An oasis is a pool of water that forms in a desert. Oases are rare and can be very hard to find.

If the aliens are looking for humans, then you need to go somewhere where very few people live. You have a few options here — the Sahara Desert in Africa, the Amazon Rainforest in South America, or — if you've packed enough sweaters — the Arctic. The easiest of these to survive in would be the Amazon. However, it's still going to be tough. But if you manage to survive in one of these places, you can lie low, meet up with other survivors, and begin your new life.

Fact: Fossil fuels can be found almost anywhere on the planet. If the aliens are looking for these resources, then almost nowhere is safe.

SURVIVING THE ALIEN INVASION

If you find yourself a remote hideout and manage to stay hidden for a long time, you might just survive the alien invasion. It's important not to lose hope. Even if us humans don't defeat all the aliens, it's likely that something else will…

The aliens will not be used to living on Earth, and this will mean that they are not used to Earth's **DISEASES**. If you are able to hide for long enough, the aliens could start getting sick — very sick. If you are lucky, the aliens will catch a deadly virus, and you will be able to lie low in your hideout while they start to drop like flies. While you wait it out, why not take up a new hobby, practice your favorite sport, or learn a musical instrument? Take some time to enjoy a quiet life, safe in the knowledge that if any more aliens set their sights on planet Earth, you'll be ready for them!

30

GLOSSARY

ADVANCED	far ahead in development
ANCIENT	belonging to the very distant past
ATMOSPHERE	the mixture of gases that make up the air and surround the Earth
BUNKER	reinforced, underground shelter
CIVILIZATION	a society that is very advanced
CULTURE	the way of life and traditions of a group of people
DISEASES	disorders that cause symptoms in a person and can make them very sick
EVOLUTION	the process by which life-forms develop from earlier forms of life
EXTERMINATE	kill and destroy completely
FOSSIL FUELS	fuels, such as coal, oil, and gas, that formed millions of years ago from the remains of animals and plants
GALAXY	many solar systems, stars, and planets that all orbit around a central point, usually a black hole
GOVERNMENT	the group of people with the authority to run a country and decide its laws
HIDEOUT	a safe building that can be used as a base
HUMANITY	all human beings collectively
INTERNATIONAL SPACE STATION	the capsule in orbit around Earth that houses astronauts from countries around the world
INVASION	an unwelcome attack on another country or planet
METEORITES	pieces of rock that successfully enter a planet's atmosphere without being destroyed
QUANTUM MECHANICS	the math and science that describe how the smallest particles in the universe work and interact with each other
RADIO SIGNALS	a type of electromagnetic wave that can travel huge distances and still be understood
REMOTE	far away from largely populated areas
STARS	giant balls of hot gas in space
TECHNOLOGY	machines or devices that are made using scientific knowledge

INDEX